the Girl Who Wanted a Song

STEVE SANFIELD

Illustrated by

STEPHEN T. JOHNSON

HARCOURT BRACE & COMPANY

San Diego   New York   London

Printed in Singapore

It all happened the summer after Marici's mother and father died.

Marici went to live with her aunt. Her aunt lived in the woods, miles from town. Her house—it was more like a cabin—sat by itself at the end of a narrow dirt road.

Each day when her aunt went to work, Marici would walk in the woods without direction. She felt alone, but she was not. The woods were home to deer and skunk, fox and bear, rabbit and raccoon. The creatures saw her and she saw them, but not a word passed between them.

Marici would often sit under the willows on the bank of the pond wondering what her life would become. She spoke to no one, and no one spoke to her.

In the early morning the peeping wrens welcomed the dawn. Other birds joined in until their songs surrounded her.

Once the sun rose above the hills, it was the frogs' turn. Hundreds, thousands, zillions of them, until it sounded like one grand symphony.

At twilight, that time that is neither day nor night, the crickets would begin to sing and sing and sing so loudly sometimes they seemed to fill the world.

And Marici thought, If only I had a song to sing.

At night when her aunt returned from work, she and Marici would sit together on the porch. Sometimes her aunt would tell Marici about the adventures she had as a young woman   her travels to Africa and the great beasts she saw there; her travels to the distant Orient with all its mysterious ways.

Some nights Marici and her aunt would read, sometimes alone, sometimes to each other. But mostly they sat silently and watched the clouds pass in front of the moon and listened to the hooting of owl and the call of coyote far off in the dark woods somewhere.

And as Marici lay in bed, waiting for sleep to come, she would again say to herself, If only I had a song to sing.

One afternoon, months after she had come to be with her aunt, Marici saw, or thought she saw, a goose scurrying from the pond into the brush.

That evening Marici asked her aunt, "Do any geese ever stay here in the summer?"

"No, my sweet. They stop here each spring on their way north and then again each fall on their way south. Why do you ask?"

"Oh, no reason really," said Marici. "I thought I saw one."

"It's not likely, since they always come in a gaggle, dozens and dozens of them, and they always leave together."

Well before dawn the next day Marici went to the pond. There was not yet enough light for her to see the lines on her own palm, but she took her place under the willow trees, determined to see the goose she thought she had seen the day before.

By the middle of the afternoon it had grown warm. Marici became drowsy and fell asleep. While she slept she dreamed deeply, and in her dream there was a goose, a large Canadian goose with a long black neck and a little white chin strap. He had black tail feathers, black feet, and tiny, bright black eyes.

The goose spoke to her in a language she had never heard before but that she understood perfectly: "I too am alone. I too need to sing, but I need someone to teach me."

"I will. I'll teach you," Marici responded, and then she awoke.

Just as she opened her eyes she saw the black and white tail feathers disappear into the brush. She was sure of it.

The next day she returned to the same spot under the willows. When the goose appeared in the afternoon, Marici called to it, "Do not be afraid. I am like you. I am alone. Maybe we can help each other."

The goose came close. They sat together and watched the sun set behind the mountains.

Day after day they would meet at the pond. The goose always came out of and returned to the brush. Marici never saw it fly, and she began to wonder why. Is it hurt? Is it afraid? Does it know how to fly?

"Why do you always stay on the ground?" she asked. "If I could fly, I'd fly everywhere. Oh, I would. I would."

And the goose answered her with a honk—a real honk. It was the first time the goose had uttered a sound. He said no more.

They sat there in silence until the sun began to set, and then they each went their own way—the goose into the brush and Marici to her aunt's cabin.

That night as she lay in her bed waiting for sleep to come, Marici thought about how the goose never flew and about how wonderful it would be to fly in the sky. Just before sleep took her mind, she began to remember a melody she had learned long ago.

The next afternoon she and the goose sat together as they did every day, and then without really thinking about it, Marici hummed the melody. When she stopped, the goose once again spoke. *"Honk. Honk. Honk, honk, honk."* Much louder and much more lively than the day before.

Just then Marici had a splendid idea. She started to sing out loud:

> *Like snow white sailing ships on a deep blue sea,*
> *High in the heavens, the clouds floating free.*

At that instant the goose began to waddle toward the pond—faster and faster as it flapped its wings until it left the earth and began to fly. Higher and higher into the blueness of the sky, honking and blaring all the way.

Marici watched the goose become smaller and smaller until it was only a jot of a dot that seemed to vanish into a cloud.

Later that night Marici told her aunt about her new friend for the first time. "He was so beautiful, Auntie, the way he flew. Oh, I wish I could fly."

"There are many ways to fly, my sweet," said her aunt. "Geese have their way. People have another."

Sure enough, that very night Marici flew. She flew in her dreams, side by side with her friend. They circled the pond and then the woods. They flew over the cabin and over the town. Sailing. Soaring. Gliding. Free. And as they flew, they sang—sometimes the goose's song: *"Honk. Honk. Honk, honk, honk,"* and sometimes Marici's song:

> *If I might fly to one,*
> *If I might glide to one . . .*

all the way to the clouds and beyond.

Marici could hardly wait to tell her friend about her dream. She went to the pond early the next day, but the goose never came. Not that day, nor the next, nor the next. Each day Marici would sit from early morning through the afternoon, and each day she remembered more and more songs from her life—the songs she loved, the songs her mother had taught her, the songs she learned at camp, the songs she used to sing with her friends, and of course, the one that gave her back her voice, the one that let the goose fly again.

She remembered and she sang. Other creatures came to the pond to drink and to listen, but not the goose.

The last red wildflowers were fading, summer was nearing its end. The smells of fall were in the air. Marici wondered if she would ever see her friend again.

Then one afternoon, no different from any other, Marici saw a dark speck high in the sky. As it drifted toward her, it grew larger, until suddenly she recognized it. It was her goose, her friend. He had returned.

She watched him come closer and closer. With his wings outstretched he glided gracefully and then landed perfectly on the smooth surface of the pond.

The goose waddled up to her, and they sat quietly side by side as they had done so often before. For a long time they shared a simple stillness, and then Marici began to sing their song. Once, twice, three times. Sometimes the goose would join in. Sometimes he would just listen.

Like snow white sailing ships on a deep blue sea
High in the heavens, the clouds floating free.

Honk. Honk. Honk, honk, honk.

If I might fly to one,
If I might glide to one,
Sailing and sailing,
What a pleasure it would be.

Honk. Honk. Honk, honk, honk.

When they finished singing, Marici and
the goose became as silent as their shadows.
They sat thinking their own thoughts until
the evening breeze began to sing its own song.

"I want to thank you," said the goose.
"Now I must go where I belong. You helped
me to fly again. Now I must join the others.
I will never forget you, sweet girl."

"And I want to thank you," Marici answered,
"for it was you who gave me back my song.
It was you who helped me to sing again.
You'll always be in my heart, beautiful goose."

And with that they each went into the world singing.

Sarah's book—S. S.

To my grandmother, Ruth I. Greenwood—S. T. J.

AUTHOR'S NOTE

十牛 *The Girl Who Wanted a Song* was inspired by the Ten Oxherding Pictures of Zen Buddhism. Those pictures tell the tale of a young boy who seeks, finds, tames, and releases an ox— and ultimately returns to the world at large. They are meant to serve as a guide to the different levels of realization leading to enlightenment and are usually painted in a circle accompanied by short commentaries and poems.

There are a number of variants, most of which originated in China during the Sung dynasty (960–1279). The earliest is a set of five pictures by Ch'ing Chou. This was expanded to six by Tzu-te Hui and finally, in the twelfth century, to ten by a Zen master of the Lin Chi school named K'uo-an Shi-yuan.

Known as Jūgyū-no-zu in Japan, where they became popular in the fourteenth century, they continue to be a source of instruction and inspiration to Zen students and others who often use them as a basis for meditation.

—S. S.

The Chinese calligraphy above represents ten ox, which is the name for the ancient pictures upon which this story is based. Calligraphy rendered by Gary Snyder.

Requests for permission to make copies of any part of the work should be mailed to:
Permissions Department, Harcourt Brace & Company,
6277 Sea Harbor Drive,
Orlando, Florida 32887-6777.

Chinese calligraphy copyright © 1996 by Gary Snyder.

Library of Congress Cataloging-in-Publication Data
Sanfield, Steve.
The girl who wanted a song/Steve Sanfield;
illustrated by Stephen T. Johnson.—1st. ed.
p. cm.
Summary: Marici, a lonely orphan, discovers that she has a song to sing when she encounters and befriends a stray Canadian goose.
ISBN 0-15-200969-8
[1. Canadian goose—Fiction. 2. Geese—Fiction. 3. Orphans—Fiction.]
I. Johnson, Stephen T., 1964–   ill. II. Title.
PZ7.S2237Gi 1996
[Fic]—dc20 95-5821

First edition
F E D C B A

The illustrations in this book were done in watercolors and pastels on Ingres paper.
The display type was hand-rendered by Georgia Deaver.
The text type was set in Perpetua.
Color separations by Bright Arts, Ltd., Singapore
Printed and bound by Tien Wah Press, Singapore
This book was printed with soya-based inks on Leykam recycled paper, which contains more than 20 percent postconsumer waste and has a total recycled content of at least 50 percent.
Production supervision by Warren Wallerstein and Ginger Boyer
Designed by Kaelin Chappell